Zanzu the Weaverbird

written and illustrated by
Elliott Friedman

Special thanks to:

Baba Wagué Diakité
Ronna Neuenschwander
Annie Moloney
Eliza Nelson
Maureen Milton
Kit Abel Hawkins

Friedman, Elliott.
    Zanzu the Weaverbird.

Summary: An original story about a bird who learns to use his talents for others, not just for himself.

Printed in the United States of America by Lightning Source, Inc.

To Arbor School and my family.

Zanzu the Weaverbird was the most talented bird living in the Baobab tree. Ever since his father had taught him to weave nests it was all Zanzu could think about. Each night, he designed nests in his dreams, and as soon as he awoke each morning, he began flying and fetching to create his latest designs. Never was his beak empty, his wings idle. No matter the nest's shape or size, Zanzu could build it. He was very proud of his homes, and he was also proud of the fact that no other birds in the Baobab tree shared his skills. Their nests were simple jumbles of twigs when compared to his creations.

Although he was very skilled and constructed the most beautiful nests, Zanzu had no friends -- no friends to compliment his work, no friends to talk to and no friends to fly with. For when the great rains came and the birds' homes became damp and weak, all the birds worked together to re-build. All that is except for Zanzu, who worked only on his own nests. And when a terrible fire came during the dry season and many birds from far away came to the Baobab tree in need of a place to stay, all the birds worked together to provide shelter for their visitors. All except for Zanzu, who would not let any other bird close to his nests. The other birds respected Zanzu's talent, but they found him to be vain and selfish.

One day Zanzu had a fantastic idea. "Maybe the other animals will admire me and speak with me if I build an enormous and magnificent home for all of them to look at and enjoy. Then I will have friends!" And so, Zanzu collected all of the strongest sticks, twigs, reeds and vines he could find and overnight Zanzu created the biggest nest any bird had ever seen. The walls were tightly woven, stronger than the scales of the largest crocodile, and Zanzu added exquisite turrets, which protruded out of the main nest. Zanzu proudly stared at what he had crafted and puffed up his bright feathers. The nest was truly perfect.

The next day, Zanzu woke early and sat atop his spectacular nest waiting for the other birds to come see his work. He waited and waited, but no one came -- not the majestic Fish Eagle, nor the mysterious Owl. Zanzu thought it was because his nest was not giant and impressive enough, so he wove the nest bigger and bigger and bigger until there were no sticks to be found for miles around. All the other birds said, "There goes Zanzu again, taking all of the twigs so that we have nothing to build with" and they turned their backs to him.

That night a great storm struck the Baobab tree. As thunder shook the sky and lightning slashed the darkness, nearly all of the birds' homes were destroyed. All, that is, except Zanzu's. The gigantic nest he had built was so strong that it survived the storm without even one twig out of place. And so, Zanzu was left as the only bird living in the Baobab tree with a nest still fully intact.

The very next day, Fish Eagle came to Zanzu's home. "My family's nest was destroyed in the storm and we have no place to sleep," he said. "Can you please let us stay with you while we try to re-build our home?"

Zanzu wanted to help Fish Eagle and his family for he admired their size and strength. But Zanzu saw the wonderful designs he had woven into the walls, and he saw the towering turrets that supported the nest. He told himself, "Surely this nest is too special to share with anyone else." And he sent Fish Eagle away.

That night, Owl came to Zanzu's nest looking extremely distressed. "Hellooo!" he called. "Zanzuuu, are yooou there? My family has nooo place to stay, and we are restless trying tooo find a place tooo sleep. Can we please stay with yooou while we try tooo make a neeew home?"

Zanzu felt sorry for Owl and wanted to help him, but Zanzu saw how expertly he had woven the thick, strong walls of his nest. And he saw how clean and organized each room was inside it, and he told himself, "Surely this nest of mine is much too special to share with anybody else." And he sent Owl away.

Many other birds came to Zanzu over the next few days, and although he had more than enough space in his nest for them to stay, he felt that protecting his palatial home was much more important than helping the other birds. And so he sent them all away.

Soon Zanzu had sent away every bird living in the Baobab tree. News of his selfishness spread from tree to tree and the other birds began avoiding him more than ever. Zanzu could not understand why, and it did not occur to him that he had done anything wrong. Zanzu sulked about in the endless passageways of his enormous nest. He was now more lonely than ever.

Zanzu had heard of a wise old bird who knew more than any animal living. It was said that he was as old as the very mountains he lived in. They called this great bird Izikulu, The Blue Crane of the Mountains, and it was Zanzu's plan to seek him out.

So Zanzu flew east, toward the mountains where his ancestors were born. He flew over the plains where the water buffalo grazed, above the mighty river where the crocodiles lurked, around the dense jungles where the monkeys swung, and he crossed the savannah where the lions roared, until the mountains finally came into sight. Then Zanzu saw him. The Blue Crane of the Mountains was standing on one leg on the top of the highest peak.

Zanzu flew to him, glad to have finally reached his destination. "Izikulu, Izikulu, Wise One, I have traveled long and far to seek your guidance."

"I have heard of your magnificent nests, Zanzu," the crane responded. "What brings you to my mountains?"

"You are right, Wise One," Zanzu said. "I am the one who builds the nests, but though they are beautiful, I have no friends and am very, very lonely."

For a while Izikulu thought. "There is a belief among us," he said. "It is as old as the sun that rises every morning. It is the belief that everything is connected, and that we are only who we are because of other creatures and how we interact with one another." Izikulu paused. "Your talent is truly impressive, Zanzu, but having skill is not enough. What matters most is how you choose to use your talent. My advice for you is to share your skills with others. That will make them happy. Then not only will you have friends, but the community will grow as well." Zanzu thanked Izikulu for his advice and began his descent from the mountain top.

Zanzu did not know what to do. And so he thought. He thought as he crossed the savannah where the lions roared, and he thought as he flew around the dense jungle where the monkeys swung, he thought as he flew over the mighty river where the crocodiles lurked, and he thought as he flew over the plains where the water buffalo grazed. Finally, an idea came to him.

That night Zanzu returned to the Baobab tree, and he began to work. First, he carefully took apart his nest, making sure he did not break one twig, reed, or blade of grass. Then, once his nest was completely dismantled, he began weaving many smaller nests from the supplies he now had. By morning, the Baobab tree was filled with new homes. In the same spot where there was once a gigantic, astonishing nest, perched the very smallest house of all. This was where Zanzu would live.

That morning, dirty from sleeping on the ground, the birds of the Baobab tree awoke to a pleasant surprise. Above them in the branches of the great tree were hundreds of nests all too beautiful to have been built by any bird but Zanzu. Fish Eagle and Owl flew up to Zanzu, who was sitting quietly on a branch near his nest. "Whose nests are these Zanzu?" asked Fish Eagle.

"Yes, Zanzuuu, are they just another one of your selfish creations?" taunted Owl.

"No," Zanzu replied. "These nests are for all the birds of the Baobab tree to live in and enjoy."

The birds were extremely thankful to Zanzu, and they asked him if they could do anything in return. All Zanzu asked for was their friendship, and they kindly obliged.

Zanzu was very happy that he now had many friends. He loved to talk with them, he loved to fly with them, and most of all he loved to build with them. He had learned the value of sharing and helping others, and as he grew older, his shared wisdom became useful to other birds. Now whenever a problem arose in the animal kingdom, Zanzu and the entire Baobab community worked together to solve it. And when they worked together like this, anything was possible. Zanzu was never lonely again.

"Umuntu Ngumuntu Ngabantu"

A Person is a Person Through Other Persons

– Zulu proverb

The guidance given by Izikulu to Zanzu in this story is based on the traditional Southern African philosophy of Ubuntu.

"Ubuntu is the essence of being a person. It means that we are people through other people. We cannot be fully human alone. We are made for interdependence, we are made for family. When you have ubuntu, you embrace others. You are generous, compassionate. You are rich so that you can make up what is lacking for others. You are powerful so that you can help the weak, just as a mother or father helps their children."

– *Desmond Tutu*

Elliott Friedman is a thirteen year old, eighth grade student living in Portland, Oregon. He has family in South Africa and looks forward to spending time there every year.

Proceeds from the sale of this book will be donated to non-profit groups focused on improving housing conditions and the lives of children in South Africa's poorest communities.

LaVergne, TN USA
03 June 2010
184856LV00001B